Level 1

Where Is My Hat?

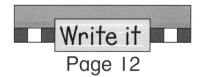
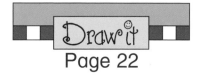
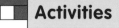

One day, Dog went for a swim.

Dog lost his red hat.

Dog went down to look for his red hat.

He saw a fish and a frog, but he did not see his hat.

Dog went up on a hill to look for his red hat.

He saw a cat and a cub, but he did not see his hat.

Dog jumped up on a box to look for his red hat.

He saw a pig and a fox but no red hat.

Dog dug and dug to look for his red hat.

He saw an ant and a bug but no red hat.

Dog was sad, but he went on
looking for his red hat.

Just then, Dog saw a skunk
with a hat. It was a red hat!

Dog smelled the skunk. Dog
smelled the hat. Yuck!

Dog went to the shop to get a new hat.

One day, Dog

went for a swim.

Dog lost his red hat.

Dog went down

to look for his red hat.

He saw a fish

and a frog, but

he did not see his

hat.

Dog went up on a hill to look for his red hat. He saw a cat and a cub, but he did not see his hat.

Dog jumped up on

a box to look for

his red hat. He saw

a pig and a fox

but no red hat.

Write it

Dog dug and dug

to look for his red

hat. He saw an

ant and a bug

but no red hat.

Dog was __sad__, but he __went__ on __looking__ for his hat.

Just then, Dog saw a skunk with a hat. It was a red hat!

Dog smelled the skunk. Dog smelled the hat. Yuck!

Dog went to the _____ _____

shop to get

a new hat.

One day, Dog went for a swim.

Dog lost his red hat.

Dog went down to look for his red hat. He saw a fish and a frog, but he did not see his hat.

Dog went up on a hill to look for his red hat. He saw a cat and a cub, but he did not see his hat.

Dog jumped up on a box to look for his red hat. He saw a pig and a fox but no red hat.

Draw it

Dog dug and dug to look for his red hat. He saw an ant and a bug but no red hat.

Dog was sad, but he went on
looking for his red hat.

Just then, Dog saw a skunk
with a hat. It was a red hat!

Dog smelled the skunk. Dog smelled the hat. Yuck!

Dog went to the shop to get a new hat.

Read it:

Go on a reading treasure hunt! For this activity, have your child or student write a simple sentence (with six or fewer words) on a piece of paper. Next, he or she should cut the sentence apart so that each word is on a separate piece of the paper. Then, he or she should hide the pieces of paper around the room. Now comes the fun part: have your child or student find the words that piece together to make a complete sentence!

Write it:

Take a poll! Have your child or student write the names of family members or friends down the left side of a large piece of blank paper. He or she should then think of a question for the poll. Then, he or she should ask each person the same question and record the answers next to their names. Kids will get lots of great writing practice taking "polls"—and they will find out lots of fun information along the way. Examples of questions: *What kind of music do you like the best? What kind of food do like the best? What is the best movie ever?*

Draw it:

Make a book of faces! This is a really fun drawing activity that your child or student can add to over time. Staple blank pieces of paper together to make a book. Then, your child or student should think of a title for the book and write it on the cover page. On each page, he or she should draw a different kind of face and write down what kind of face it is. (Examples: a happy face, a sad face, a mad face, a silly face, a sleepy face, a surprised face, a chicken pox face, a dirty face.) Then, ask your child or student to read the book out loud.

A NOTE TO THE PARENTS:
When children create their own spellings for words they don't know, they are using **inventive spelling**. For the beginner, the act of writing is more important than the correctness of form. Sounding out words and predicting how they will be spelled reinforces an understanding of the connection between letters and sounds. Eventually, through experimenting with spelling patterns and repeated exposure to standard spelling, children will learn and use the correct form in their own writing. Until then, inventive spelling encourages early experimentation and self-expression in writing and nurtures a child's confidence as a writer.